How Will I Get to School This Year?

Jerry Pallotta

SCHOLASTIC INC.

David Biedrzycki

To Lucia Fraser, Maura White, and Katie McEachern,
three great teachers!

— J.P.

To Mr. Paul Brennan and my friends at
Riverside Elementary West, Taylor, PA,
my hometown. How will you get to school this year?

— D.B.

ISBN 978-0-545-37288-6
Text copyright © 2011 by Jerry Pallotta
Illustrations copyright © 2011 by David Biedrzycki
All rights reserved. Published by Scholastic Inc.
SCHOLASTIC and associated logos are trademarks and/or
registered trademarks of Scholastic Inc.
12 11 10 9 8 7 6 5 4 3 2 1   13 14 15 16 17/0
Printed in the U.S.A.   40
This edition first printing, July 2013

WELCOME BACK
STUDENTS
SCHOOL STARTS
WEDNESDAY WE
ARE LOOKING
FORWARD TO A
GREAT SCHOOL
YEAR

RIVERSIDE W
ELEMENTARY SCHOOL

School starts tomorrow.

Last year, I got tired of taking the smelly school bus

What if I went to school a different way?

I'll ride on a giant mosquito.

What will my classmates think?

A pig will provide a good ride.

I'll hog the highway.

Maybe flying on a bald eagle is faster.

Meet me at the flagpole!

I'll swing to school on a gorilla.

I don't mind banana breath.

Yippee! I could float to school.

A zillion butterflies will flap their wings for me.

I'll swim to class on a hammerhead.

But where will I park the shark?

Who needs a bus?

I'll be riding a giant tarantula.

I can walk to school. No bullies will bother me.

I'll be protected by a pride of lionesses.

OFFICE

ALL GRIZZLIES
AND VISITORS
MUST REPORT TO THE
OFFICE AND SIGN IN

I can sit back and relax.

It's sweet to be delivered by two grizzlies.

I could hop to school with a family of frogs.

Did they forget their backpacks?

I could commute in the mouth of a white tiger.

Uh-oh! She thinks she's my mother.

Could a tortoise get me to school on time?

I wouldn't want to miss lunch.

There are many ways to get to school.
But it's more fun when I go with my friends.

The school bus is here!

I love school. I can't wait to go back.